The Mop and Dad at the Top

PHASE 2

1a

Level 1 – Pink

Helpful Hints for Reading at Home

The graphemes (written letters) and phonemes (units of sound) used throughout this series are aligned with Letters and Sounds. This offers a consistent approach to learning whether reading at home or in the classroom. Books levelled as 'a' are an introduction to this band. Readers can advance to 'b' where graphemes are consolidated and further graphemes are introduced.

HERE IS A LIST OF NEW GRAPHEMES FOR THIS PHASE OF LEARNING. AN EXAMPLE OF THE PRONUNCIATION CAN BE FOUND IN BRACKETS.

Phase 2			
s (sat)	a (cat)	t (tap)	p (tap)
i (pin)	n (net)	m (man)	d (dog)
g (go)	o (sock)	c (cat)	k (kin)
ck (sack)	e (elf)	u (up)	r (rabbit)
h (hut)	b (ball)	f (fish)	ff (off)
l (lip)	ll (ball)	ss (hiss)	

HERE ARE SOME WORDS WHICH YOUR CHILD MAY FIND TRICKY.

Phase 2 Tricky Words			
the	to	I	no
go	into		

HERE ARE SOME WORDS THAT MIGHT NOT YET BE FULLY DECODABLE.

Challenge Words			
Dan's			

TOP TIPS FOR HELPING YOUR CHILD TO READ:

• Allow children time to break down unfamiliar words into units of sound and then encourage children to string these sounds together to create the word.

• Encourage your child to point out any focus phonics when they are used.

• Read through the book more than once to grow confidence.

• Ask simple questions about the text to assess understanding.

• Encourage children to use illustrations as prompts.

PHASE 2

1a

This book is an 'a' level and is a pink level 1 book band.

The Mop
and
Dad at the Top

Written by
Gemma McMullen

Illustrated by
Jasmine Pointer

Can you find 5 objects in the picture below which start with the letter m?

The Mop

Written by
Gemma McMullen

Illustrated by
Jasmine Pointer

It is Sam.

It is Sam and Tim.

Sam and a pot.

Tip it in!

Tip it in!

Tip it in!

It is a dog.

MIX IT

Dan the dog.

MIX IT

FLOUR

The dog and the pot.

Dog in the pot!

Sam and a mop.

Dan on the mat.

Can you say this sound and draw it with your finger?

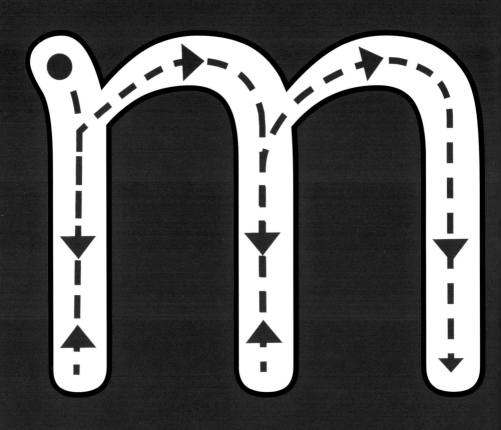

Dad at the Top

Written by
Gemma McMullen

Illustrated by
Jasmine Pointer

It is Dan.

It is Dan's dad.

Dan is in the pit.

Dad is at the top.

It is Mat the cat.

Go to Dan, Mat.

Mat can dig in the pit.

Not in the pit, Mat.

It is Sam the dog!

Sit, Sam the dog!

Dad is not at the top!

©2020 **BookLife Publishing Ltd.**
King's Lynn, Norfolk PE30 4LS

ISBN 978-1-83927-271-4

All rights reserved. Printed in Malaysia.
A catalogue record for this book is available
from the British Library.

The Mop & Dad at the Top
Written by Gemma McMullen
Illustrated by Jasmine Pointer

An Introduction to BookLife Readers...

Our Readers have been specifically created in line with the London Institute of Education's approach to book banding and are phonetically decodable and ordered to support each phase of the Letters and Sounds document.

Each book has been created to provide the best possible reading and learning experience. Our aim is to share our love of books with children, providing both emerging readers and prolific page-turners with beautiful books that are guaranteed to provoke interest and learning, regardless of ability.

BOOK BAND GRADED using the Institute of Education's approach to levelling.

PHONETICALLY DECODABLE supporting each phase of Letters and Sounds.

EXERCISES AND QUESTIONS to offer reinforcement and to ascertain comprehension.

BEAUTIFULLY ILLUSTRATED to inspire and provoke engagement, providing a variety of styles for the reader to enjoy whilst reading through the series.

AUTHOR INSIGHT:
GEMMA MCMULLEN

Gemma McMullen is one of BookLife Publishing's most multi-faceted and talented individuals. Born in Newport, Gwent, she studied at the University of Northampton, where she graduated with a BA (Hons) in English and Drama. She then attended the University of Wales where she obtained her PGCE Primary qualification, and has been teaching ever since. Her experience as a teacher enables her to find exactly what makes children focus and learn, and allows her to write books that amuse and fascinate their readers.

PHASE 2

1a

This book is an 'a' level and is a pink level 1 book band.